THE PRINCE'S BREAKFAST

To my fellow Fussy Eaters. This one's for us! — J. O.
To Seb and Leon, who both love ketchup! — M. L.

Barefoot Books
2067 Massachusetts Ave
Cambridge, MA 02140

Barefoot Books
29/30 Fitzroy Square
London, W1T 6LQ

First published in the United States of America by Barefoot Books, Inc
and in Great Britain by Barefoot Books, Ltd in 2014
This paperback edition first published in 2019

Audiobook narrated by Hugh Bonneville
Recorded, mixed and mastered by
Sans Walk Spoken Word Studio, England
Graphic design by Judy Linard, London, UK
Reproduction by B & P International, Hong Kong
Printed in China on 100% acid-free paper

This book was typeset in Fontesque Bold 24 on 33 point
The illustrations were prepared in acrylic paints and pencils

Paperback ISBN 978-1-78285-417-3

British Cataloguing-in-Publication Data:
a catalogue record for this book is available from the British Libr

Library of Congress Cataloging-in-Publication Data is availabl
under LCCN 2015029606

1 3 5 7 9 8 6 4 2

Go to *www.barefootbooks.com/princesbreakfa*
to access your audiobook online.

THE PRINCE'S BREAKFAST

Written by
Joanne Oppenheim

Illustrated by
Miriam Latimer

Narrated by
Hugh Bonneville

Barefoot Books
step inside a story

In a faraway kingdom, a long time ago,
When breakfast was served, the Prince shouted, "NO!"

He turned up his nose at omelettes with cheese.
He pooh-poohed the porridge,
though his mother said, "Please!"

He sipped his hot chocolate; he ate his toast dry.
But to all other offerings, he said, "No, not I."

"Alas," said the Queen to her husband the King,
"How can he grow when he won't eat a thing?"

The King stirred his tea; then after one sip,
"I have it!" he said. "We shall go on a trip!"

The very next day, preparations were started,
And in less than a week, the royal household departed.

They journeyed in style to the city of Agra.
"Our idlees are moist," beamed the grand maharajah.

His chef steamed the rice cakes, with chutney on top.
The King started eating and just couldn't stop.

"So good!" he declared. "Have a taste, boy — just try."
But the Prince shook his head and said, "No, not I."

"Perhaps," said their host, "a dosa will do.
We can fill it with dahl or potatoes for you."

The Queen took one forkful; the King sampled two.
"Delicious," they said. "Just try a few!"

"The spices are perfect; come, don't be shy."
But the Prince shook his head and said, "No, not I."

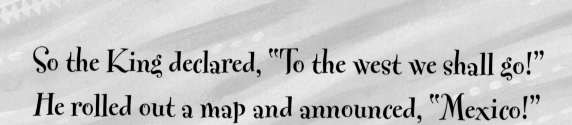

So the King declared, "To the west we shall go!"
He rolled out a map and announced, "Mexico!"

On the pier, people shouted, "Hello! ¡Buenos dias!"
And welcomed them warmly with trays of tortillas,

Fried eggs, avocados, salsa and cheese.
"¡Por favor!" said the King,
"I'll have more, if you please!"

"Muy bien," said the Queen. "Why don't you try?"
But the Prince shook his head and said, "No, not I."

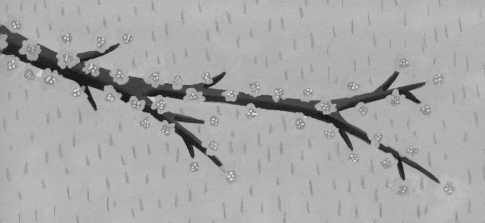

"What shall we do now?" the Queen asked with a sigh.
"My dear," said the King, "We shall go to Shanghai."

They stayed at the home of a rich mandarin.
"My chefs," he declared, "can indulge every whim."

"We've prepared a fine breakfast we hope you'll enjoy.
There is something for everyone — even your boy!"

"Does the Prince care for congee? Here: try a pot
With our very best pickles." The King ate the lot.

"This thousand-year egg will make the Prince strong.
It will bring him good fortune and help him live long."

"Yes, indeed!" said the King. "Come now, have a try."
But the Prince shook his head and said, "No, not I."

That night in his room the King sat up in bed. "We'll take him to Zambia — that's it!" he said.

"A safari will give him a HUGE appetite.
Oh fal-lal-lal-lah! I KNOW I am right!"

The Prince loved adventures!
He met his first giraffe.
It licked the King's crown and
made them all laugh.

He woke up a lion
that gave a great roar;
Then closed its eyes tight
and continued to snore.

He met herds of zebra and wild wildebeest.
"And now," said the King, "It's time for our feast!"

Their breakfast was served on beautiful leaves,
With freshly fried plantain and fruit from the trees.

At the sight of fresh fruit, the Prince sealed his lips tight.
The King was dismayed. He said, "This is not right!"

"This plantain is perfect," the Queen said. "Do try."
But the Prince shook his head and said, "No, not I."

The Queen was distraught. "Let's go home," she sighed.
"Our boy is still picky...whatever we try."

Just as she said this, a bright-eyed old man
Said, "Perhaps I can help. I believe that I can."

Then he pulled a red bottle from deep in his case,
Winked at the Prince and said, "Fancy a taste?"

"What's this?" asked the Prince. "It smells so delicious!"
"Oh dear," frowned the Queen. "Are you sure it's nutritious?

"I think," said the man, "there's no cause for alarm.
A dash of this ketchup will do him no harm."

"I eat it with everything, from rhubarb to rice."
"Mmmm" said the Prince. "It tastes really nice!"

He poured it on pancakes; he spread it on bread.
The King was so happy he stood on his head.

The Queen gave a twirl
and a trill of delight.
Their banquet continued
all day and all night.

From that morning on, whatever he ate,
The Prince added ketchup and cleaned up his plate!